87x 9/20

Dora in the Deep Sea

by Christine Ricci
illustrated by Robert Roper

Ready-to-Read

Simon Spotlight/Nick Jr.

New York   London   Toronto   Sydney   Singapore

SIMON SPOTLIGHT
An imprint of Simon & Schuster Children's Publishing Division
1230 Avenue of the Americas, New York, New York 10020
Copyright © 2003 Viacom International Inc.
Manufactured in the United States of America
16 18 20 19 17 15
Library of Congress Cataloging-in-Publication Data
Ricci, Christine.
Dora in the deep sea / by Christine Ricci ; illustrated by Robert Roper.—1st ed.
p. cm.— (Dora the explorer ready-to-read ; #3)
"Based on the TV series Dora the Explorer(tm) as seen on Nick Jr."
Summary: Dora and Boots go down deep into the sea in a submarine to help Pirate
Pig find his lost treasure chest. Features rebuses.
ISBN-13: 978-0-689-85845-1 (pbk.)
ISBN-10: 0-689-85845-0 (pbk.)
1. Rebuses. [1. Buried treasure—Fiction. 2. Marine animals—Fiction. 3. Rebuses.]
I. Roper, Robert, ill. II. Dora the explorer (Television program) III. Title. IV. Series:
Ready-to-read. Level 1, Dora the explorer ; #3.
PZ7.R355 Dl 2003
[E]—dc22
2003010523

Hi! I am . This is .

DORA　　　　　　　　　　　**BOOTS**

And here is our friend,

. looks sad.

PIRATE PIG　　**PIRATE PIG**

What is wrong, ?

PIRATE PIG

"I have lost my !"

TREASURE CHEST

says 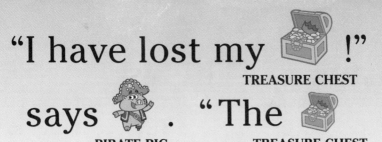 . "The

PIRATE PIG   **TREASURE CHEST**

fell off my 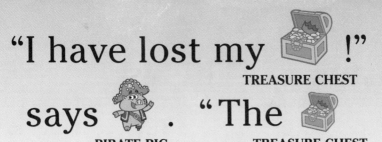 and

SHIP

into the !"

SEA

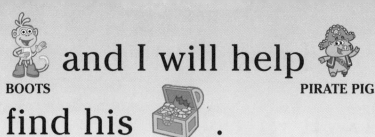

BOOTS and I will help **PIRATE PIG**

find his  .

TREASURE CHEST

Will you help too?

We need something to take
us down into the  .
SEA

What can take us into the

SEA ?

A 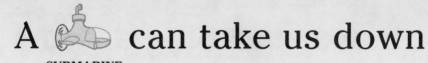 can take us down
SUBMARINE
into the ![sea] !
SEA

Ooh, we are going down into the  .

SEA

Look! A  !

SAND CASTLE

Hello, !

KING CRAB

There is a  FISH with SPOTS

by the ROCK .

I see a 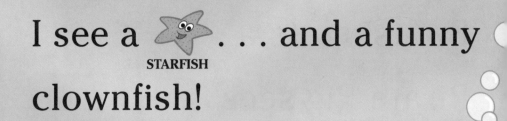 . . . and a funny

STARFISH

clownfish!

Boots spots a  **GREEN TURTLE**.

Pirate Pig sees **YELLOW SEA HORSES**.

Oh, no! Here come some

 !

LOBSTERS

They will try to pinch

the  with their !

SUBMARINE   CLAWS

We drove the  **SUBMARINE**

past the **LOBSTERS** !

Now we need to find

the **TREASURE CHEST** .

Hooray! We found the  !

TREASURE CHEST

But we have to watch out

for 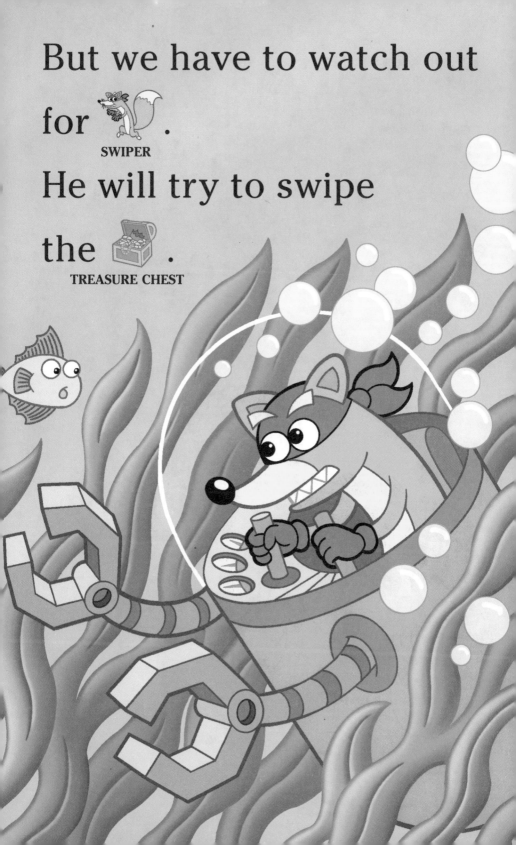 .

SWIPER

He will try to swipe

the 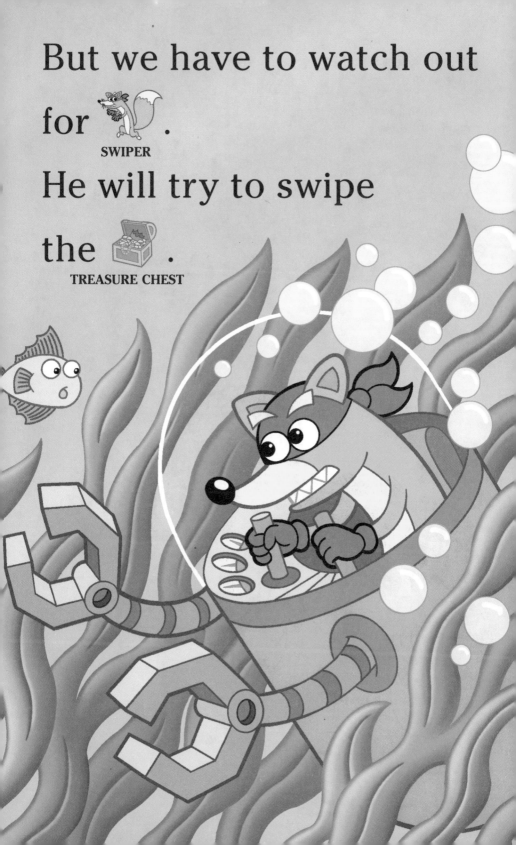 .

TREASURE CHEST

Do you see  ?

SWIPER

Look! is behind the !

SWIPER

WHALE

He is going to swipe

the !

TREASURE CHEST

We have to say " , no swiping!"

SWIPER

You helped us stop !

Yay! 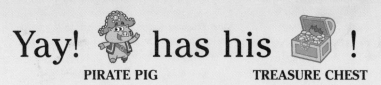 has his  !

PIRATE PIG **TREASURE CHEST**

Thank you for helping!